T is for Torture

Marie Lestrange

To all the freaks who dare to be their authentic, spooky selves— this book is for you.

*Disclaimer: This novel is fiction, except for the parts that aren't.

Printed in Oliver Springs, Tennessee, United States of America
Library of Congress Control Number: 2023935855

Description: Crimson Cult Media, 2023 | 32 pages of 4-color illustrations. | Series: Little Lestrange. | Audience: Adult. | Summary: Little Lestrange learns about the dark side of history by examining torture devices from A to Z.
Identifiers: LCCN 2023935855| ISBN: 979-8-9880338-0-6 (hardback) | ISBN: 979-8-9880338-1-3 (paperback) | ISBN: 979-8-9880338-37 (ebook)
Subjects: FICTION_HORROR, WIT AND HUMOR| Picture Books. |.BISAC: FIC015000, FIC016000, TRU010000

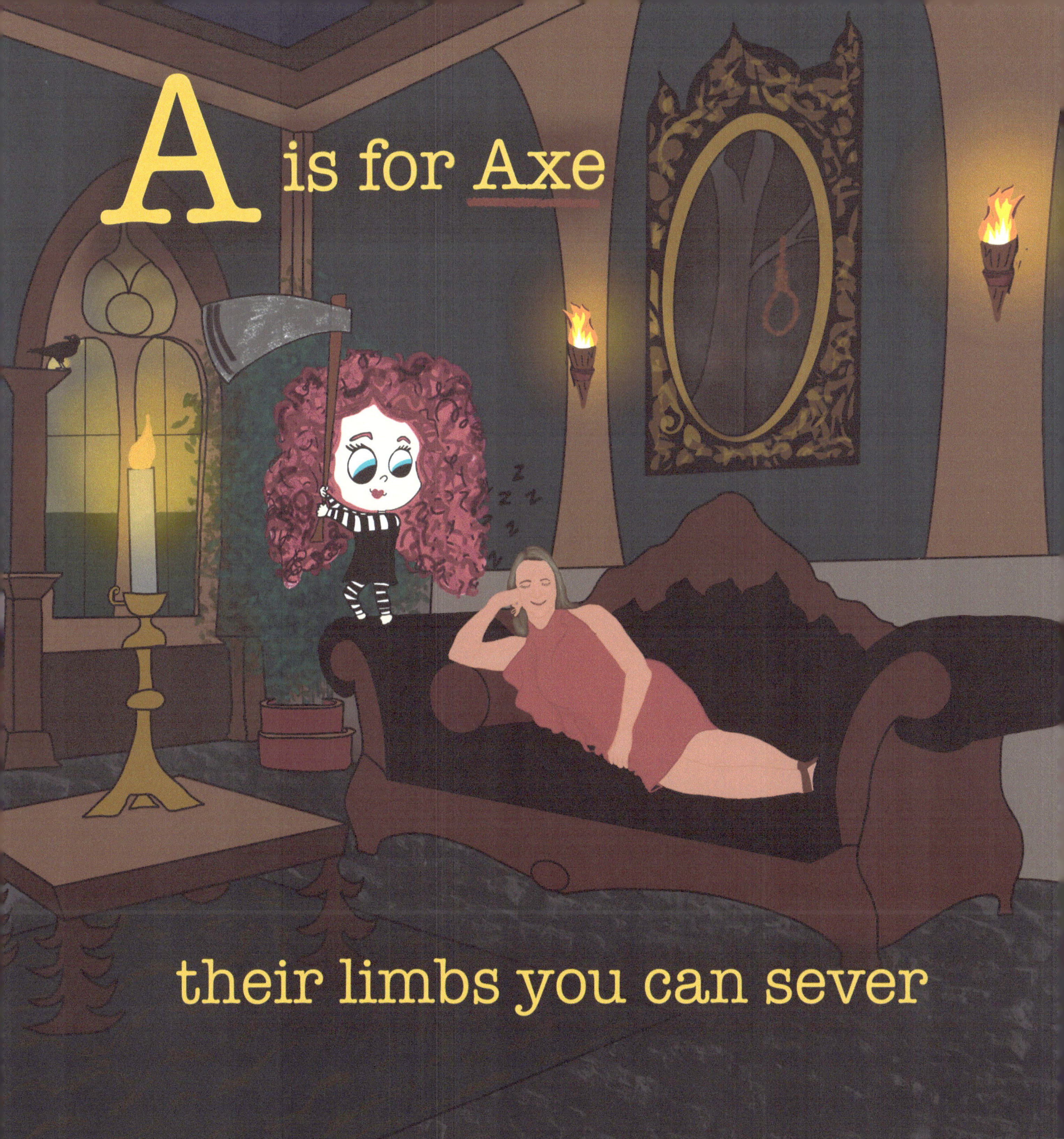

A is for Axe
their limbs you can sever

B is for
Breast ripper 
a painful endeavor

C is for Cattleprod,

which comes with a shock

D is for Ducking stool,
much worse than the stock

Welcome
Disorderly
Women

E is for Exposure

often buried alive

F is for Flaying,
impossible to survive

G is for Gibbeting,

left alone to die

H is for Heretic's fork,

they'll confess to

any lie

I is for Iron Maiden

spiked with nails
on all sides

J is for
Judas Cradle,
a pointed edge
they'll sit astride

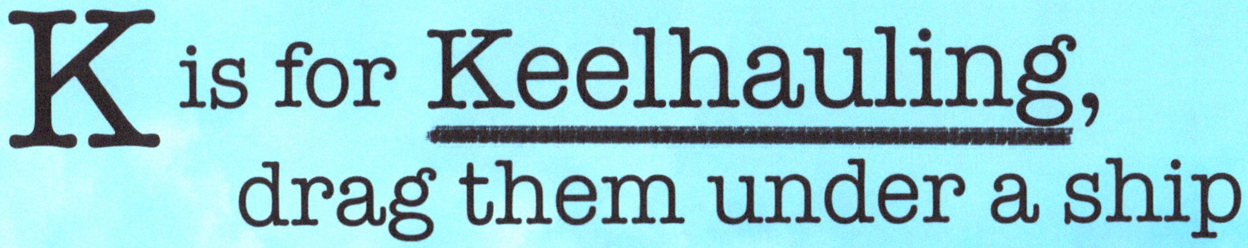

K is for <u>Keelhauling</u>,
drag them under a ship

L is for Lead Sprinkler,
molten metal you can drip

M is for Malay Boot,
to crush the foot or leg

N is for Nero's Roman candles

Burning while they beg

O is for Oil (boiled, that is!)
with a pulley, cauldron, and hook

P is for Pillory,
so all the town can look

Q is for Quartering,

torn limb from limb

R is for Rats,

their escape quite grim

S is for Scaphism,

a nasty affair

T is for The Rack 
this one
is fair

U is for Upended Sawing,
the blood leaves a trail

WELL SHIT

V
is for
Vlad
you, too, can impale!

W is for Breaking Wheel,

the pain is quite severe

X is for eXploitation,
clowns are her worst fear

Y is for Yawn,
no sleep is now his doom

Z is for the worst of all,
an endless meeting in ZOOM!